Usborne English Readers
Level 3

Oliver Twist

Retold by Mairi Mackinnon
Illustrated by Elena Selivanova

English language consultant: Peter Viney

Contents

You can listen to the story online here:
www.usborneenglishreaders.com/
olivertwist

In a small English town, some distance from London, a baby was born. His life began, not in a comfortable home or a hospital, but in the workhouse – a horrible place where the poorest people lived, because they had nowhere else to go.

"Let me see him before I die," whispered his mother.

"Die? You're not going to die," said the doctor, but he was wrong. The mother closed her eyes and lay still.

"She's a good-looking girl," said the doctor. "Where did she come from?"

"Nobody knows," said the nurse. "They found her in the street last night. She had obviously walked a long way. Her shoes were in pieces."

"She won't need them now," said the doctor.

"She won't need this, either," said the nurse. She took something from around the woman's neck, and put it in her pocket.

So the child's mother was dead, and nobody knew who his father was.

"Another orphan!" complained Mr. Bumble, the manager of the workhouse. "Well, he needs a name. He can be Oliver – we don't have an Oliver. And his surname… we are up to T in the alphabet. Oliver Twist, he shall be. Now, he's too young to stay here. We'll send him out to the country until he is older."

For the next eight years, Oliver lived in the country with twenty other orphans. It was a simple life. The children had very little food and very few clothes. Sometimes they became ill, or had accidents, and died. It didn't change anything: there were always more orphans.

But Oliver was still alive eight years later, so he came back to the workhouse. If he was hungry before, he was hungrier now. He had three meals a day, and they were always the same: one small bowl of watery porridge. He shared a large, cold bedroom with eleven other boys.

"Porridge, always porridge!" they said one night. "It's not enough."

"We should ask for more – but who dares ask?"

"Oliver, you're new. You can do it."

The next day, the boys finished their porridge in less than a minute. Oliver took his bowl to Mr. Bumble.

"Please, sir, I want some more."

Mr. Bumble was shocked. "MORE? You wicked boy! We can't keep greedy, lazy boys like you." He put a notice on the workhouse door: BOY NEEDS WORK. WILL PAY £5.

That afternoon, a tall, thin man came to the workhouse. His name was Mr. Sowerberry, and he made coffins. "More coffins for you, Mr. Bumble? More deaths? The workhouse is an unhealthy place, isn't it? Oh, and let me see this boy."

Oliver came in. He looked frightened.

"He's very pale, very small… but I'll take him."

"Why do we need another boy?" asked Mrs. Sowerberry. "We already have Noah – and boys eat a lot."

"This one won't," said Mr. Sowerberry.

Noah gave Oliver a bowl with some small pieces of dry meat. "It's the dog's dinner. He didn't want it." Oliver ate hungrily, and Noah laughed.

Mr. and Mrs. Sowerberry left the room. "Dog boy," laughed Noah, "born in the workhouse. I suppose your mother was no good."

"Don't talk about my mother!" said Oliver.

"I knew it!" said Noah. "She –"

"Stop!" Oliver jumped up and pushed Noah. The bigger boy fell on the ground and started screaming. "Help! Murder! The new boy attacked me!" "They'll put you in prison," he told Oliver. "Maybe you'll die."

Oliver didn't wait to see what happened next. He ran into the street and through the town. When he was too tired to run, he walked, and finally he stopped. Then he saw a sign.

"London!" he said. "It's a big city. Nobody will find me there." Every day, he walked as far as he could. At night, he slept in the fields. He walked for seven days, and in all that time only two people gave him a little bread.

He reached the edge of the city on the eighth day. He was too tired and hungry to walk any further, and he sat down to rest.

Oliver realized that a strange boy was watching him. He was wearing a man's coat and hat, and the hat was almost falling off his head. Then the strange boy crossed the road and spoke.

"Are you new here?" Oliver nodded. "I thought so. No money? Nowhere to sleep? Come with me." First the strange boy took him to a pie shop. Oliver thought the hot pie was the best meal of his life. "They call me the Artful Dodger," said the boy. "Artful, because I'm clever, and Dodger – well, you know what dodging is?" Oliver wasn't sure, but he didn't say so. "I have a kind old friend. If I ask him, he'll give you a place to stay, and you won't even have to pay him."

"That *is* kind," said Oliver. He followed
Dodger through the streets. They passed
tall houses and busy shops. Then the streets
became narrower and more crowded, and finally
Dodger opened a door and led Oliver up some
dark and dirty stairs to a large, smoky room.

"Hey, Fagin! Meet my new friend, Oliver
Twist."

Through the smoke Oliver saw four or five
other boys, and an old man with red hair and
a red beard. The old man gave Oliver a huge
smile. "Well, isn't this nice? You must have
dinner with us, Oliver, but before that we'll
play a little game."

The old man put things in all the pockets of his long coat, and then he turned around. The boys had to walk up quietly behind him, and try to take the things out. If the old man noticed, they lost. All the boys thought this was very funny.

"Now, Oliver, would you like to try?"

"I don't think I can do it, sir."

"Don't worry. You will, my boy, you will."

After dinner, two young women came in. Their names were Bet and Nancy. Oliver thought they looked nice, but rather untidy.

"Who's your new boy, Fagin?" asked Nancy.

"My dears, this is Oliver. He's visiting from the country. I hope he'll stay with us for a *long* time," said Fagin, and the other boys laughed.

"Oh, Fagin, you won't get him into trouble, will you?" asked Nancy. "He looks too good for you."

"Exactly, my dear," said Fagin quietly. "He looks so innocent. Nobody will suspect him of anything."

A few days later, Fagin said, "Dodger, you must take Oliver out today. I believe he needs some air."

Dodger and another boy took Oliver to a little square, where they saw a well-dressed man outside a bookseller's. The man picked up a book and started reading. "Perfect," said the Dodger. He and the other boy moved closer, then they put their hands in the man's pockets and ran away.

FINE BOOKS

Oliver was shocked. "But that's stealing!" So that was what his new friends did. They were pickpockets! Suddenly the man put his hands in his pockets, and turned around. "Stop thief!"

Everyone stared at Oliver, then started
running towards him. Oliver looked around,
but he couldn't see the other boys anywhere.
He was terrified, and he started running
too. A huge crowd was chasing him…
and then he fell, and heard a loud voice:
"Police! Where's the thief?"

"Wait!" It was the well-dressed man.
"I really don't think it was this boy. Does
he have my things?"

The policeman looked in Oliver's pockets.
"Nothing here," he said, "But maybe he
dropped them."

"Sir," said another voice, "I saw everything.
This good man was looking at my books when
two other boys came and robbed him. They ran
away before everyone started chasing this boy."

"He doesn't look well," said the first man.
"We have frightened him, and he may be hurt.
My name is Mr. Brownlow. I'd like to help him."

Oliver didn't remember much about arriving at Mr. Brownlow's house, except that it was very big and grand. The next morning, he woke in a clean, comfortable bed. A lady was smiling at him.

"Am I dead? Am I in heaven? he asked. "Are you an angel?"

"Oh my dear child, no. I'm Mrs. Bedwin, the housekeeper. Do you feel better? Then sit up and try to eat a little soup." Later, she gave Oliver some new clothes.

"Oh, they're too good for me," he said, but he put them on.

"Don't be silly, dear, you look like a..."

"…like a picture! Come with me, dear." She took Oliver's hand and led him downstairs to a study full of books. Mr. Brownlow was sitting there at his desk. On the wall was a picture of a young lady. "Mr. Brownlow, sir, do you see?"

Mr. Brownlow looked from the picture to Oliver and back again. "Incredible! Oliver, do you recognize this lady?"

"No, sir," said Oliver. "She's very beautiful, and she has a kind face. Who is she?"

"Who *was* she, you mean… Oliver, my boy, where were you born?"

In Fagin's large, smoky room, there was another visitor. He was a big, dangerous-looking man with a rough-looking white dog. Even the Dodger looked nervous.

"Where's the new boy? How did you lose him, you stupid fools?"

"Calm down, Bill," said Fagin. "We'll find him."

The big man threw a cup at Fagin, but it missed. Nancy put a hand on his arm, but he shook it off. "Make sure you do. If he tells the police, we're finished."

"I have heard something." Fagin opened a parcel, and held up Oliver's old clothes. "A friend of mine bought these this morning from a big house in Islington..."

"Then get him back! I can't go there, and you can't, but Nancy will go. Let's hope he hasn't talked already."

Mr. Brownlow was showing Oliver the books in his study. "Do you like reading, Oliver?"

"Oh, yes sir. I'd like to read all of these!"

There was a knock at the door. Mrs. Bedwin brought in a parcel, and Mr. Brownlow opened it. "Look, these are from the bookseller where I first met you. But wait, is he still here? I have some others to give back to him."

"He's gone, sir, just five minutes ago."

"I am sure I could go after him," said Oliver. "I'd like to help."

"Thank you, my boy." Mr. Brownlow gave Oliver the books and some money, and he left the house. He ran as fast as he could.

Suddenly two strong arms caught him. "Oliver! My dear little brother! Please come home. Mother is so worried."

"Nancy! Let me go! I'm not your brother!"

"What are you saying? Oh, Oliver, you'll break your mother's heart." Everyone in the street was looking at Oliver and shaking their heads. Nancy was holding him so tightly that he couldn't escape.

"Dear child," said Fagin. "You weren't really planning to leave us?"

"Books!" said a boy. "You won't need these."

"Money!" said another. "You're so kind!"

"Nice clothes!" said the Dodger, pulling them off Oliver. "Let's not get them dirty."

Oliver started crying. "They belong to Mr. Brownlow!"

"Ah, but Mr. Brownlow doesn't need them now," said Fagin, "and we do."

"But he'll think I'm a thief!"

"You are," said the big man, "so be quiet."

"Oliver, you haven't met Mr. Sikes,"
said Fagin. "Bill is a very good friend of
ours, but we mustn't make him angry."

Sikes was looking at Oliver. "He's very
thin. I can use a thin boy. That house, Fagin,
you know, that big place with all the silver...
A thin boy is exactly what we need."

"Bill, no!" said Nancy "It's too dangerous!"

Sikes looked at her angrily. Oliver
thought he was going to hit her.

For three days, Oliver wasn't allowed to leave the smoky room. When Sikes or Fagin or the boys weren't there, they left Sikes's dog Bullseye with him. Oliver was almost as frightened of Bullseye as of Sikes.

On the third evening, Sikes said, "We're going out." He showed Oliver a gun. "You know what this is for? It's to make sure you stay quiet, do you understand?"

They walked a long way through London. The night was dark and the streets were empty. Sikes didn't speak, but every time Oliver looked at him, he could see the gun in his hand.

At last they reached a big house near the river. Sikes took Oliver to the back of the house, and showed him a high, narrow window. Then he lit a lantern, and pushed the window open.

"I'm going to put you through here, and give you this lantern," he told Oliver. "You're going to take it to the front door, and open it for me. I'll watch you all the way. If you make a sound, I'll shoot, do you hear?"

Oliver was terrified. He nodded. Then he was inside the house, with the lantern.

"I can't let Bill steal from these people," he thought. As he reached the front door, he heard a sound from upstairs. "Hurry!" said Sikes' voice from outside. Oliver opened the door and dropped the lantern at the same time.

"Stop!" shouted another voice, and a gun fired from somewhere above him. Oliver felt a sharp pain in his arm, and he fell to the ground.

Sikes kicked the door open, and everyone stopped talking.

"What happened?" asked Fagin.

"Disaster," said Sikes. "That stupid boy woke everyone up."

"Oliver? Where is he?" asked Nancy.

"I had to leave him there," said Sikes. "Someone shot him. I'm lucky that they didn't shoot me, too. Now, give me something to eat." After his meal, he took off his boots and went to sleep in a corner.

Nancy quietly put on her hat, but Fagin noticed. "Nancy, my dear," he said. "Are you going out?"

"I need some air," she said. "Sssh, don't wake Bill."

"Watch where she goes," Fagin whispered to the Dodger. "Don't let her see you."

Mr. Brownlow had a visitor.

"I... I know you don't usually talk to people like me," said Nancy, "but please listen. You want to help Oliver, don't you? I hope it's not too late."

"Oliver?" asked Mr. Brownlow. "Where is he? Is he all right?"

Nancy explained about Sikes and the big house. "Bill wanted Oliver to climb in and open the door for him. He knew they had silver and jewels. Then it all went wrong, and Bill ran away and left him there. I just hope he wasn't badly hurt," she said.

"I'll go there immediately," said Mr. Brownlow. "Will you come with me?"

"I can't," said Nancy. "I must go back. My friends are bad people, it's true, and Bill is probably the worst. But I can't help it – I love him."

"You're a brave girl," said Mr. Brownlow. "If ever I can help you, please come back to me."

Sikes was awake, and angry. "Where's my Nancy?"

"Ah," said Fagin. "She went out, but the Dodger followed her. I'm not as stupid as you think."

"No," said Sikes, "you're even more stupid. She's gone to the police, you old fool."

Just then, the Dodger came back. "It's all right, Bill. She went to that rich old man, the one who gave Oliver those new clothes."

"Then *he'll* go to the police!" shouted Sikes.
"Don't you understand anything?" He ran out
into the street, towards Mr. Brownlow's house.
Bullseye ran after him.

Sikes soon saw Nancy, who was on her way back.

"Bill, what's wrong?"

Sikes dragged her into a narrow street, then
through a broken door into a ruined house.

"Bill, what are you doing?" Nancy was terrified. She tried to run past Sikes, but he picked up a heavy piece of wood and stood in her way.

"You told him where to find us!"

"I didn't! Bill, please! I promise!" Nancy put her hands up, and Sikes swung the piece of wood. It hit her head, and she fell on to the ground.

"Nancy... No!" Sikes looked away. "I didn't mean to kill her!" he cried. Bullseye started howling, and Sikes kicked him. The white dog ran away.

Mr. Brownlow was in the sitting room of the big house. He was talking to Mrs. Maylie, the owner. "So is he getting better?" he asked. "You have been very kind."

"We didn't think that he looked like a thief," said Mrs. Maylie. "The doctor has seen him, and he is asleep now. My servant is very sorry that he fired the gun. *I* am sorry that we didn't catch the other man."

"I am sure the police will catch him soon," said Mr. Brownlow. "The most important thing is that Oliver is safe. As soon as he is well again, I'll take him home with me. By then, I may have some more news. You see, I think I know who he is."

Sikes waited in the ruined house until it was dark. Sometimes he thought that the body on the floor was still moving, but he knew he was imagining it. He sat where he couldn't see Nancy's pale face. At last he left the house. He stayed in the shadows, and didn't look at people's faces.

Before he reached the dark and dirty stairs, he realized that something had happened. There was a small crowd, pointing and shouting. "Thieves! Prison is too good for you!" In a moment, he saw some policemen dragging Fagin and his boys away. Now where could he go? He had no gun, no money and no food. He had left everything in Fagin's room.

He passed a window, and saw a face in the glass. It was Nancy's face! He looked again, and it was gone.

He walked this way and that, through the streets. Sometimes he saw a woman's red dress or a hat, just like Nancy's... but when he looked again, they weren't like hers after all.

At last he lay down under a bridge to sleep. As he closed his eyes, he saw her face again. "Leave me alone!" he cried.

Sikes slept badly. In his dreams, he went back again and again to the ruined house and the body on the floor. Sometimes the body stood up, and sometimes it spoke. By the morning, Sikes was cold and hungry, and he ached all over. He got up and started walking. He had some friends in an old house near the river, he remembered. He would go there.

He saw a poster on the wall.

He didn't need to read any more. He started running.

The houses near the river were almost as ruined as the one he had left. They reminded him… but he couldn't think about that. There were people running after him now, more and more. Suddenly a white shape ran out of the crowd. "Bullseye!" shouted Sikes. "How did you find me? Go away! Leave me alone!"

"That's the murderer!" someone said. Sikes ran up the stairs to his friends' house. "Open the door!" he shouted.

"We don't want you here," they shouted back.

"You have to help. If you don't help me, they'll smash this place."

Someone opened the door and gave him
a rope. Sikes climbed up to the roof of
the house. He tied one end of the rope
to the chimney, and made a loop in
the other. Some of the crowd were
starting to climb the stairs after him.
Now, if he could put the loop around
his body, and climb down behind
the house, away from the crowd…

Sikes put the loop over his head,
and looked up and saw –

"It's her face!" he screamed.
"Her eyes!" He slipped and fell,
and the loop pulled tightly
around his neck.

In a small English town, some distance from London, a well-dressed man was visiting a workhouse.

"I'd like to ask about a boy," he said. "A boy named Oliver."

"Oliver?" Mr. Bumble thought for a moment. "Oh yes. A wicked, greedy, lazy boy. A criminal boy, I'm sure." Suddenly he noticed the boy standing next to Mr. Brownlow. "Erm, I mean…"

"Can you tell me about his mother? Can anyone tell me?"

"I don't know anything," said Mr. Bumble. "I wasn't there, and the doctor is dead now. Ah, but there was the nurse…"

The nurse looked at Oliver. "He's like the little picture," she said.

"The little picture?" asked Mr. Brownlow.

The nurse opened a wooden box and pulled out a necklace. "I know it wasn't right to take it," she said, "but I kept it safe, didn't I?"

On the necklace was a gold ring and a picture of a young man. Mr. Brownlow pointed to a name inside the ring: AGNES.

"Oliver, my dear boy," he said. "That is a picture of your father. Do you remember the lady in the picture at my house? Her name was Agnes. She was the daughter of my oldest friend, and she was your mother. Your father died many years ago, and I never knew what happened to your mother after that. But oh, my boy, I am so happy that I have found you at last."

About Charles Dickens

Charles Dickens was born in 1812, the second child in a large family. His father was a generous man, but he spent more money than he earned. When Charles was ten, he had to leave school and work for ten hours a day in a factory to help his family. He never forgot what it was like to be poor. When he grew up, he worked as a news reporter, and he began to write short stories.

Oliver Twist was Dickens's second long book. It was originally published in twenty-four parts, in a magazine, between 1837-1839. The story was a huge success. Readers were fascinated by the details of Oliver's early life, and shocked at the terrible things that happened to him. Dickens described criminals like Fagin, Sikes, Nancy and the Artful Dodger in a realistic and unromantic way, but he also told an exciting story.

Dickens wrote fifteen books, as well as plays, many shorter stories, newspaper articles and hundreds of letters. His books and letters helped to change laws and improve thousands of lives, especially for children and poor people.

Activities

The answers are on page 48.

The story begins

Can you put these pictures and
sentences in the right order?

A.

Oliver took his bowl
to Mr. Bumble.

B.

"Hey, Fagin! Meet my new
friend, Oliver Twist."

C.

"He needs a name. Oliver
Twist, he shall be."

D.

"London!" he said.
"It's a big city. Nobody
will find me there."

E.

"Dog boy!" laughed Noah.
"Born in the workhouse."

F.

"You're not going to
die," said the doctor,
but he was wrong.

Who's who?

Find *two* sentences that describe
each character.

Dodger   Oliver   Mrs. Bedwin

A.
Fagin doesn't
want to make
him angry.

B.
He has a study
full of books.

C.
She calls Oliver
her "dear little
brother".

D.
He has a dog
called Bullseye.

E.
Her friends are
bad people.

F.
He asks for
more porridge.

Nancy

Sikes

Mr. Brownlow

G.

Oliver thinks she's an angel.

H.

He knew Oliver's mother.

I.

He takes Oliver to Fagin.

J.

He buys Oliver a hot pie.

K.

She brings Mr. Brownlow a parcel.

L.

He runs away from Mr. Sowerberry.

Missing words

Choose a word from the list to finish each sentence.

"It's a .... city. Nobody will find me there."

"A .... boy is exactly what we need."

thin

anxious

big

smoky

"Nice clothes! Let's not get them ...."

"I'm not as .... as you think."

brave

dirty

glad

"I hope it's not too ...."

"You're a .... girl."

stupid

cruel

late

Stop, thief!

Choose the right sentence for each picture.

1.

a) The boys had to talk
   quietly behind him.

b) The boys had to walk up
   quietly behind him.

2.

a) They put their hands in the
   man's pockets and ran away.

b) They put their hands in the
   man's pockets and looked away.

3.

a) Then Oliver was inside the
   house, with the lantern.

b) Then Bill was inside the
   house, with the lantern.

4.

a) He saw some policemen dragging
   Fagin and his boys away.

b) He saw some policemen dragging
   Bill and his boys away.

Word list

ache (v) to feel pain or hurt.

angel (n) people believe that angels are good
and powerful beings that live in heaven.

artful (v) clever and good at getting what you want.

chimney (n) something on top of a building
that lets out the smoke from a fire.

coffin (n) the wooden box that dead people are buried in.

disaster (n) a terrible event, or an event which goes badly wrong.

dodge (v) to avoid something, or to avoid doing something.

drag (v) to pull something slowly along the ground.

fire (v) to shoot a gun.

heaven (n) a lovely place where people believe you go when you die.

housekeeper (n) someone whose job is to
manage a house and the servants in it.

howl (v) when a dog howls, it makes a long sad noise.

lantern (n) a light that you can carry, often with a candle inside.

loop (n) when you put one piece of string or
rope over another in a circle, you make a loop.

manager (n) someone in an organization who tells people what to do.

mile (n) a measurement of distance. 1 mile = 1.6 km.

murder (n, v) an illegal killing. If you murder someone, you
kill them on purpose when they are not fighting you.

necklace (n) something that you wear around your neck. It is often made of gold, silver or jewels.

orphan (n) a child whose parents are dead.

parcel (n) when you want to send something to a person, or carry several things together, you might make a parcel.

pickpocket (n) someone who steals things from people's pockets.

pie (n) a kind of food made with meat, vegetables and pastry.

porridge (n) a cheap food made with oats (a type of seed) and hot water.

poster (n) a large piece of paper on a wall, showing information or a picture.

rob (v) to steal from a person or an organization.

ruined (adj) if something is ruined, it is completely broken or spoiled.

study (n) a special room in a house that is used for reading and working.

unhealthy (adj) if something is unhealthy, it is not good for you and can make you sick.

well-dressed (adj) wearing smart and expensive clothes.

workhouse (n) a place in 19th-century Britain where poor people could have a little food and a place to sleep, but they had to work hard at unpleasant jobs.

Answers

The story begins
F, C, A, E, D, B

Who's who?
Dodger – I, J
Oliver – F, L
Mrs. Bedwin – G, K
Nancy – C, E
Sikes – A, D
Mr. Brownlow – B, H

Missing words
1. big
2. thin
3. dirty
4. stupid
5. late
6. brave

Stop, thief!
1. B
2. A
3. A
4. A

You can find information about other
Usborne English Readers here:
www.usborneenglishreaders.com

Designed by Hope Reynolds
Series designer: Laura Nelson Norris
Edited by Jane Chisholm
With thanks to Laura Cowan
Digital imaging: John Russell

Page 40: picture of Charles Dickens © Mary Evans Picture Library.

First published in 2017 by Usborne Publishing Ltd.,
Usborne House, 83-85 Saffron Hill, London EC1N 8RT, England.
www.usborne.com Copyright © 2017 Usborne Publishing Ltd.